A a B b C c D d E e

F f G g H h I i J j

K k L M M m N n O o

P p Q q R r S s

V v W w X x Y y Z z

D1455934

A a B b C c D d E e

F f G g H h I i J j

K k L M M m N n O o

P p Q q R r S s T t U u

V v W w X x Y y Z z

A STEP-BY-STEP DRAWING BOOK

D is for DOODLE

Deborah Zemke

oodles
of doodles
from
A to Z

Blue Apple Books

To John

Copyright © 2004 by Deborah Zemke

CIP Data is available.
Published in the United States 2004 by
🍎 Blue Apple Books
515 Valley Street, Maplewood, N.J. 07040
www.blueapplebooks.com
Distributed in the U.S. by Chronicle Books

First Edition
Printed in China
ISBN: 1-59354-029-9
3 5 7 9 10 8 6 4

D is for Doodle

Doodling is a way of taking your mind for a walk. You can start anywhere--

with a line... /

or a squiggle... ～

or a shape... ◯

The doodles in this book all start with letters of the alphabet--and lots of letters start with a shape, like...

a circle...

O C G Q

or a triangle...

△ ▽ ∧ V W

or a rectangle.

▢ E F H

Some other doodle shapes you'll be using...

Teardrop   **Bean**   **Curlicue**   **Swoop**

Arcs are parts of circles.

Slices are different parts of circles.

Trapezoids have four sides like rectangles, but two of the sides slant in different directions. A wedge is a rounded trapezoid.

Wedge

Wave...and wavy line   Ziggy line   Squiggly line

Doodle hands are made of loops...

Let's get started. Remember, with doodling, you can start anywhere--with A or B or Z!

These A's have altitude!

1) Draw a sideways A.

2) Add four curls...

3) three bumpy lines...

4) legs with claws...

5) six curved lines...

6) eyes and teeth.

A is for Alligator

1) Draw two a's.

2) Connect them at a point...

3) and put them on a big fat a.

4) Draw four lines with red feet...

5) four wavy lines...

6) and thirteen green a's
with dots for eyes.

a is for alien

B is for Butterfly

1) Draw a B...

2) sliding down a hill.

3) Add an i...

4) and a curly v...

5) three 3's...

6) and another curly V.

There's a B in this lady's bonnet.

It's the flight of the humble bumble B!

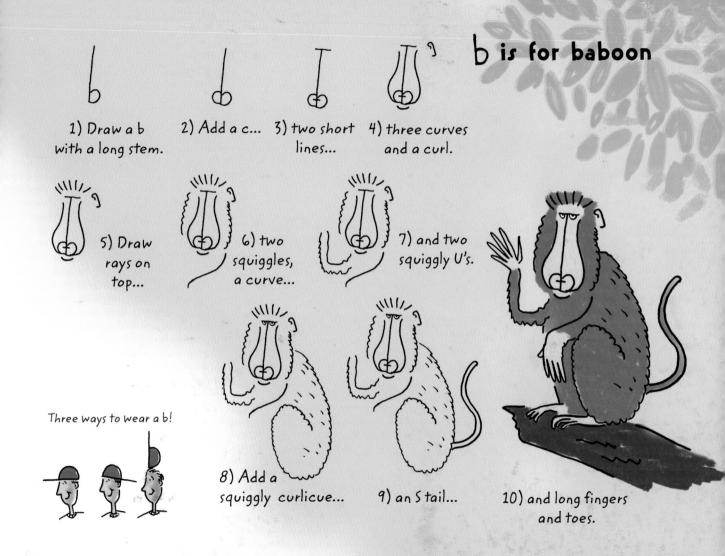

b is for baboon

1) Draw a b with a long stem.

2) Add a c...

3) two short lines...

4) three curves and a curl.

5) Draw rays on top...

6) two squiggles, a curve...

7) and two squiggly U's.

8) Add a squiggly curlicue...

9) an S tail...

10) and long fingers and toes.

Three ways to wear a b!

C is for Clown

1) Draw three C's. 2) Add two more C's... 3) six curves... 4) and two red triangles with C's on top.

5) Add squiggles... 6) hands and feet... 7) five more C's... 8) and a seat!

C is for crab

Look up! There's a comet streaking across the sky!

How many c's do you see in this cloud?

These caterpillars are c's on feet!

1) Draw a c...

2) and a backward c.

3) Add two fat triangles...

4) eight skinny ones...

5) and ten trapezoids.

6) Draw ten more triangles...

7) two ziggy V's...

8) claws and eyes. Be careful--I pinch!

D is for Dome

1) Draw a D lying down.

2) Put an i on top.

3) Add a squiggle between three straight lines....

4) on top of a triangle...

5) on top of five bars...

6) on top of a trapezoid.

7) Add a roof, walls...

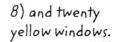

8) and twenty yellow windows.

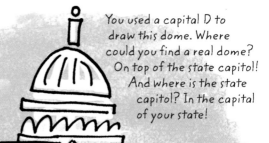

You used a capital D to draw this dome. Where could you find a real dome? On top of the state capitol! And where is the state capitol? In the capital of your state!

1) Draw four swinging d's.

2) Make two big waves, one of them upside down.

3) Add a small black T...

4) two o's with dots...

5) two flying teardrops...

6) and three slices.

7) Run, Spot, run!

E is for Elephant

1) Draw two E's lying down.

2) Attach three curves.

3) Add a small slice on a stem...

4) a curvy C...

5) and another slice.

6) Draw a striped J...

7) a curvy line on top...

8) and squiggle toes.

e is for elf

1) Draw two e's.

2) Attach three V's...

3) and two
more V's,
upside down.

4) Add five curls...

5) squiggle hands...

6) eyes, mouth, stripes,
and suspenders.

1) Draw an F.

2) Attach a C.

3) Add a bean...

4) three triangles...

5) and three dots.

6) Make rows of squiggles...

7) legs and...

8) the tip of the tail.

These flags are flying.

F is for Fox

1) Draw an f.

2) Add two dotted 0's...

3) a falling f...

4) and two S's.

5) Attach two curves...

6) another f...

7) and a squiggle wing.

8) Draw two y's...

9) a J and an l.

10) Finish the legs and walk in the water.

This f is fishy!

f is for flamingo

G is for Grandpa

1) Draw a G.

2) Make a face of two O's, a C, and a J.

3) Add a rounded M...

4) two topsy-turvy V's...

5) a W and some hair, but not too much.

6) Give Grandpa hands and feet...

7) twinkling eyes and a dotted bow tie.

Gee! The goose is loose!

1) Draw a long g.

2) Add a half ziggy line...

3) a c and a dotted i.

4) Attach a big speckled bean.

5) Draw a teardrop ear and tail...

6) three sideways waves...

7) a skinny W...

8) four wedge hooves and more speckles.

g is for giraffe

H is for Hats

1) Draw an H.

2) Add a squiggle...

3) and a face.

1) Draw an H.

2) Add loopy curves...

3) and a face. Howdy partner!

Try these funny hats on for size, then doodle your own cool hat.

Hey! This one flies!

h is for helicopter

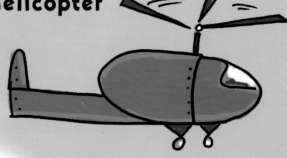

1) Draw an h lying down.

2) Attach a D....

3) and a P lying down.

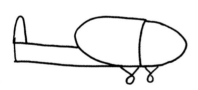

4) Add two v's and two o's...

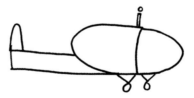

5) a dotted i...

6) and three skinny triangles to take off!

I is for Impala

1) Draw an I.

2) Attach two tears with stems.

3) Add a rounded V and two small c's...

4) and four striped slices on top.

5) Draw a big swoopy curve...

6) and a long curvy line.

7) Add two S's...

8) three sideways waves...

9) and a W.

1) Draw two i's...

2) on top of an O.

3) Add two dotted O's.

i is for insect

4) Attach a small W.

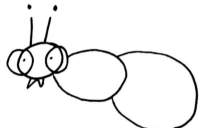

5) Add two big O's...

6) three i's leaning left...

7) and six i's upside down.

Here's a bright idea!

I scream for ice cream!

Insects rule! There are more insects than any other creature on earth--and they all have six legs, no more and no less.

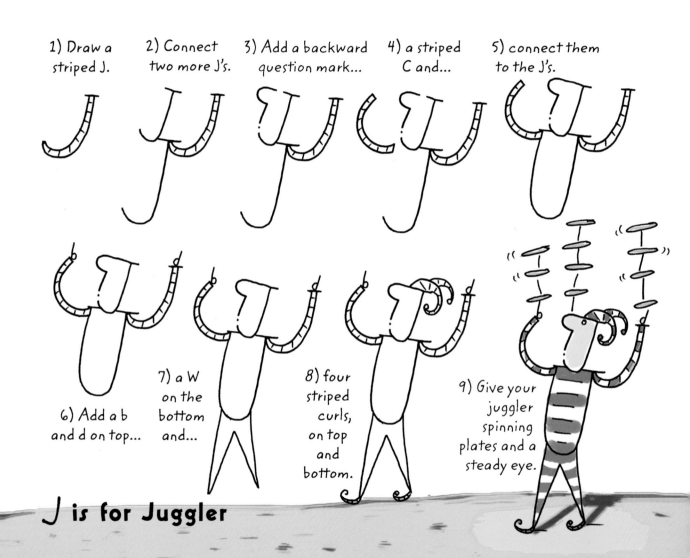

1) Draw a striped J.

2) Connect two more J's.

3) Add a backward question mark...

4) a striped C and...

5) connect them to the J's.

6) Add a b and d on top...

7) a W on the bottom and...

8) four striped curls, on top and bottom.

9) Give your juggler spinning plates and a steady eye.

J is for Juggler

1) Draw four swinging j's.

2) Make four squiggle paws...

3) and attach three big waves.

4) Attach a U...

5) a question mark...

6) and connect them with a swoop.

7) Draw a slanted Y on a black T...

8) two V's, a double curve, two small o's...

9) and swirly spots.

j is for jaguar

1) Draw a leaning K.

2) Add two curly V's...

3) two question marks...

4) two 2's...

5) and four tears.

6) Attach a big C...

7) then draw curly toes, eyes, and nose.

K is for Kangaroo

1) Draw a k.

2) Attach a triangle...

3) and a curlicue...

4) a C with curlicues..

5) two triangles...

6) and four v's.

7) Give the knight a lance...

8) and a horse.

K is for knight

L is for Lion

1) Draw a leaning L.

2) Add a d and a triangle...

3) rows of squiggly mane...

4) seven L's and a 2...

5) connected by a bean.

6) Now add a tail with a tear...

7) four loopy paws...

8) and teeth!

l is for lighthouse

1) Draw an l.

2) Add three slanted l's.

3) Top them with five little l's.

4) Add a triangle on top...

5) six little boxes and a small o...

6) and six rays of light.

M is for Monster

1) Draw an M.

2) Connect the ends with a smile.

3) Add two palm trees...

4) an O with teeth...

5) two beady eyes...

6) blue fur...

7) and running feet!

Head for the Mountains!

m is for mouse

1) Spell the word-- start with m...

2) add an O...

3) and a U...

4) a skinny S...

5) and an e.

6) Now add eyes, feet, whiskers...

7) and some tasty cheese!

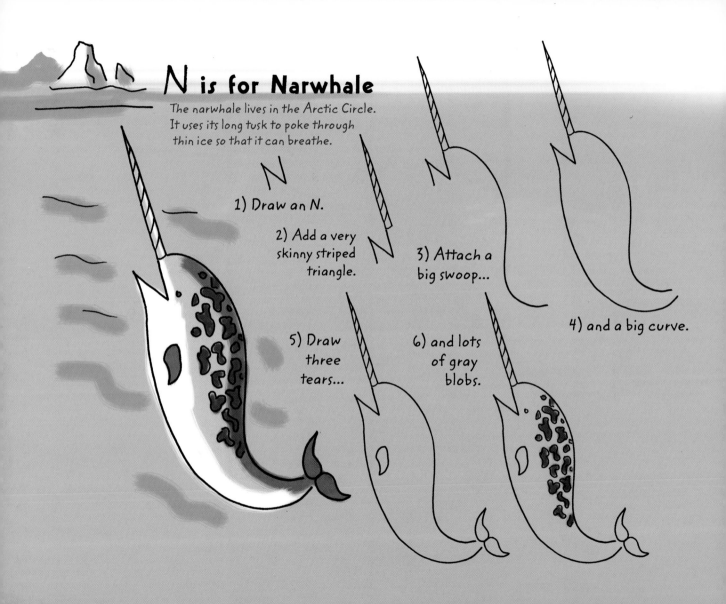

N is for Narwhale

The narwhale lives in the Arctic Circle. It uses its long tusk to poke through thin ice so that it can breathe.

1) Draw an N.

2) Add a very skinny striped triangle.

3) Attach a big swoop...

4) and a big curve.

5) Draw three tears...

6) and lots of gray blobs.

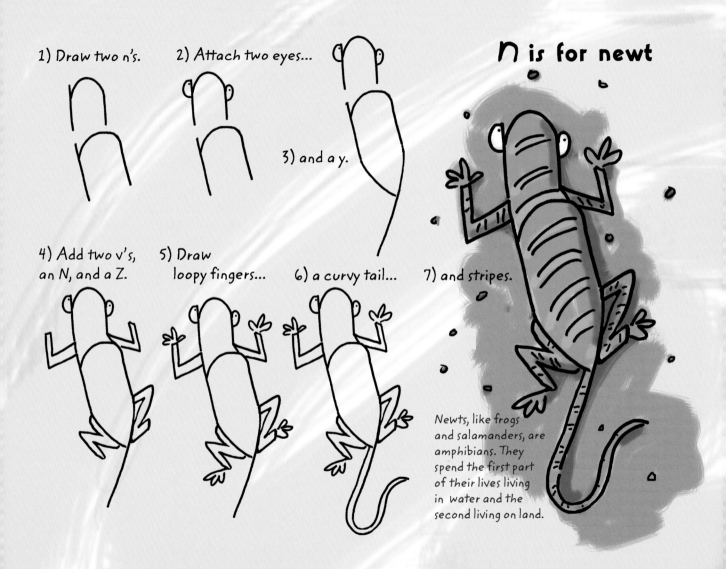

1) Draw two n's.

2) Attach two eyes...

3) and a y.

n is for newt

4) Add two v's, an N, and a Z.

5) Draw loopy fingers...

6) a curvy tail...

7) and stripes.

Newts, like frogs and salamanders, are amphibians. They spend the first part of their lives living in water and the second living on land.

O is for Ogre

1) Draw an O.

2) Add a dotted O and two little o's...

3) a curlicue...

4) a tear with teeth...

5) and two curly S's.

6) Attach a big O.

7) Draw two hairy slices with fat fingers...

8) and two fat slices with hairy toes.

9) Now make your ogre hairier and scarier and green.

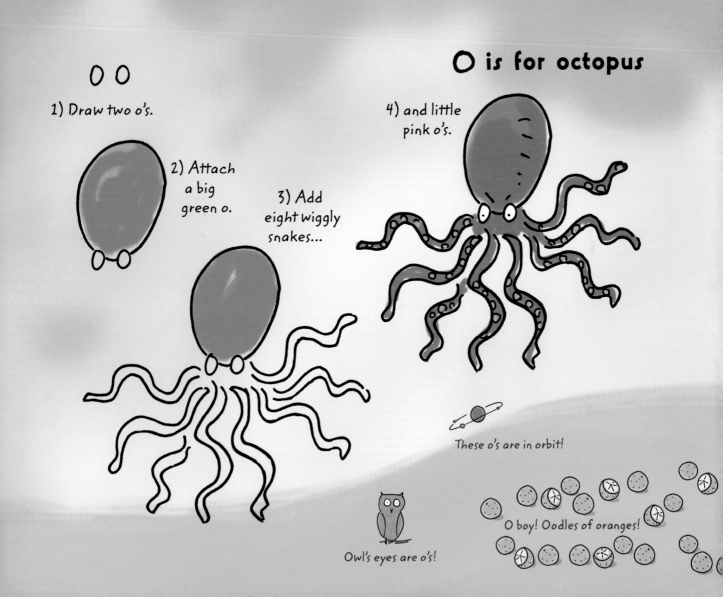

O O

1) Draw two o's.

O is for octopus

2) Attach a big green o.

3) Add eight wiggly snakes...

4) and little pink o's.

These o's are in orbit!

O boy! Oodles of oranges!

Owl's eyes are o's!

P is for People

It's fun to turn P's into people.

1) Start with a P and then...

2) put the eyes on top

or

2) put the eyes inside.

3) Give your person glasses.

Hey! What about us? We're P's too!

4) Give your person cool glasses.

5) Make your person sing.

6) Make your person swing.

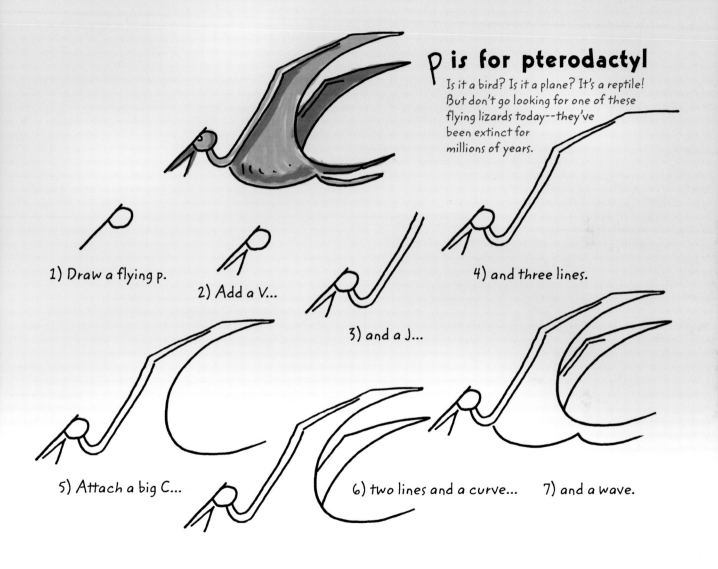

p is for pterodactyl

Is it a bird? Is it a plane? It's a reptile! But don't go looking for one of these flying lizards today--they've been extinct for millions of years.

1) Draw a flying p.

2) Add a V...

3) and a J...

4) and three lines.

5) Attach a big C...

6) two lines and a curve...

7) and a wave.

Q is for Quarterback

1) Draw a Q. 2) Add a striped trapezoid...

3) and a big fat T.

4) Draw a square W...

5) two L's...

6) a hand holding a football...

7) and a hand pointing to a touchdown.

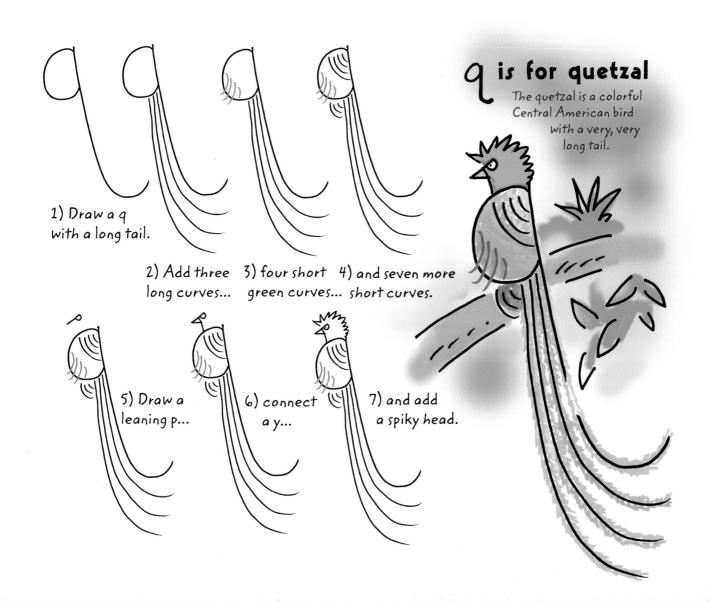

1) Draw a q with a long tail.

2) Add three long curves...

3) four short green curves...

4) and seven more short curves.

5) Draw a leaning p...

6) connect a y...

7) and add a spiky head.

q is for quetzal

The quetzal is a colorful Central American bird with a very, very long tail.

R is for Rabbit.

1) Draw a slanted R...

2) and an L...

3) and a 2.

4) Add a squiggly ball...

5) two teardrops and a sideways V...

6) and two dots, white and black.

7) Draw a paw...

8) and give your rabbit a carrot to gnaw.

r is for robot

1) Draw an r.

2) Add an upside down cup with two handles.

3) Make a robot arm with circles and rectangles.

4) Make another arm.

5) Draw another upside down cup without handles.

6) Add a bunch of small circles...

7) a ziggy neck...

8) and radio antennae.

9) Now watch your robot go!

1) Draw a fat swoopy S.

2) Attach two striped curves.

3) Add squiggle hands...

4) and a U.

5) Use five curves to draw a face.

6) Add a b lying down...

7) and two beans.

8) Add four swirl wheels and go!

S is for Skateboarder

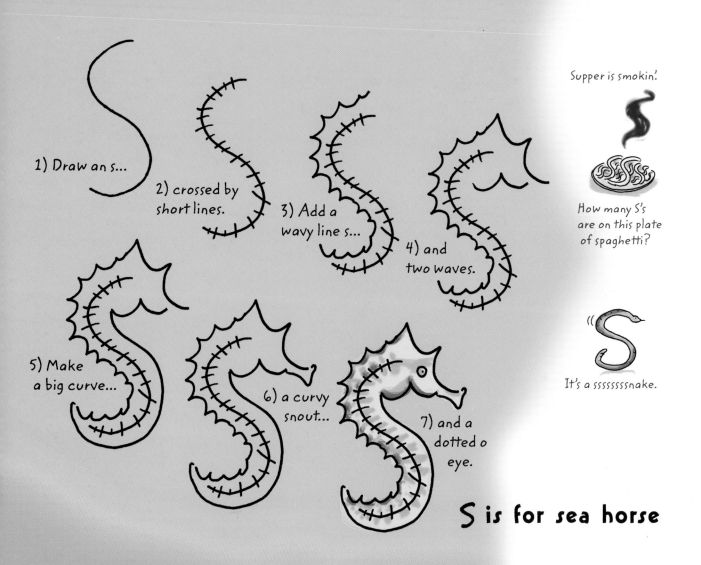

1) Draw an s...

2) crossed by short lines.

3) Add a wavy line s...

4) and two waves.

5) Make a big curve...

6) a curvy snout...

7) and a dotted o eye.

Supper is smokin'.

How many S's are on this plate of spaghetti?

It's a sssssssnake.

S is for sea horse

T is for Tyrannosaurus Rex

The biggest meat eater of all time, Tyrannosaurus Rex grew to twenty feet tall. Its head was six feet long.

1) Draw six tiny T's...

2) and six more, upside down.

3) Add a 7 and two curlicues...

4) a T and...

5) a question mark.

6) Draw a bumpy curve and a smooth curve.

7) Add two curlicue arms, two S legs...

8) ziggy toes and a swoopy tail.

1) Draw a t.

2) Put a box with a rounded top around it.

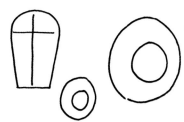

3) Add a big O and a little O...

4) and draw squiggle curves inside.

5) Attach two J's, one upside down and one sideways.

6) Add a square C and a round C...

7) and six t's.

8) Now finish with a steering wheel and seat.

t is for tractor

U is for Umbrella

1) Draw a fat U.

2) Attach four U's on the top and...

3) a little U on the bottom.

4) Draw four waves.

5) Add an l.

6) Put an upside down U on the top.

7) Now pick it up and turn it around before you get wet!

The umpire says, "Safe!" but the UFO is out of there!

U

1) Draw a u.

2) Add a skinny striped triangle...

3) and a small black triangle.

4) Attach a C...

5) and a striped slice.

U is for unicorn

6) Draw a wide u...

7) and a sideways S.

8) Add four tail S's...

9) and four V legs with wedge feet.

Found in old fables and stories, the unicorn has a horse's body and a single horn in the center of its forehead.

V is for Venus's-flytrap

Here's a plant with bad table manners. When an insect comes by, the leaves of the flytrap snap shut and hold the insect until it's been digested.

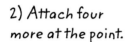

1) Draw a V.

2) Attach four more at the point.

3) Top with five curvy V's...

4) and on top of those put five hearts.

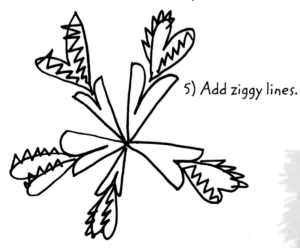

5) Add ziggy lines.

6) Now wait patiently for lunch to fly by.

∨ is for vampire bat

1) Draw two v's.

2) Add an upside down heart...

3) inside another upside down heart.

4) Draw two v's on sticks.

5) Hang your bat from a branch and finish with three small o's and fur.

Hey dude! Cool vest!

The volcano Vesuvius is erupting!

Will you be my Valentine?

W is for Wizard

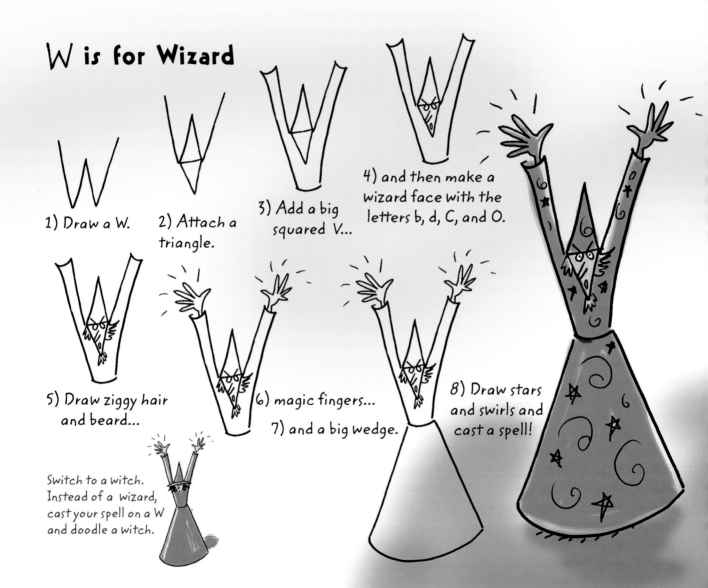

1) Draw a W.

2) Attach a triangle.

3) Add a big squared V...

4) and then make a wizard face with the letters b, d, C, and O.

5) Draw ziggy hair and beard...

6) magic fingers...

7) and a big wedge.

8) Draw stars and swirls and cast a spell!

Switch to a witch. Instead of a wizard, cast your spell on a W and doodle a witch.

W is for walrus

1) Draw a tall skinny w.

2) Top it with an upside down wave.

3) Add a question mark...

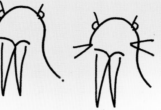

4) one d and one b...

5) two sideways V's...

6) and a big J.

7) Now make flippers with four curly V's.

1) Draw an X.

2) Put a slanted L on top...

3) and a striped rectangle on top of that.

4) Add another X...

5) and draw a V inside a Y.

6) Draw five V's, four O's...

7) shades and a nose.

8) Now add two feet to a dancing beat.

X is for Xylophone

1) Draw an x...

2) and connect the ends.

3) Add an arrow.

4) Connect with curves.

5) Add five triangles...

6) stripes...

7) a row of x's...

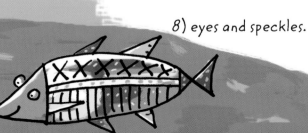
8) eyes and speckles.

You can actually see inside this transparent fish. But you have to take a really close look because x-ray fish are only two inches long.

X is for x-ray fish

Y is for Yeti

Some people have reported seeing a hairy, humanlike creature, also known as the Abominable Snowman, high in the Himalayas.

1) Draw a Y...

2) with two beady eyes...

3) a tuft of fur on top...

4) and six furry rows below.

5) Add two curvy Y's...

6) two upside down Y's...

7) more fur...

8) fingers, toes, and snow!

Y is for yo-yo

1) Draw a y with a long tail.

2) Attach an O.

3) Add four curls...

4) a bow...

5) and a striped J.

6) Draw a striped trapezoid...

7) a squared W...

8) and a self-portrait.

1) Draw two Z's.

2) Connect the sides.

3) Draw a zigzag on top...

4) and put a 7 around it.

5) Add zigzag hair and beard...

6) four more Z's...

7) two arms...

8) and zap! a lightning bolt.

Zeus is the king of gods in Greek mythology and the master of thunder and lightning.

Z is for Zeus

This Z can zoom!

1) Draw six skinny z's.

2) Add two question marks.

3) Put an S on one...

4) and two teardrops on the other.

5) Draw a swervy S...

6) four skinny striped V legs...

7) with wedge feet.

8) Add a ziggy mane, stripes...

9) and eight blue z's. Good night, zebra!

Z is for zebra

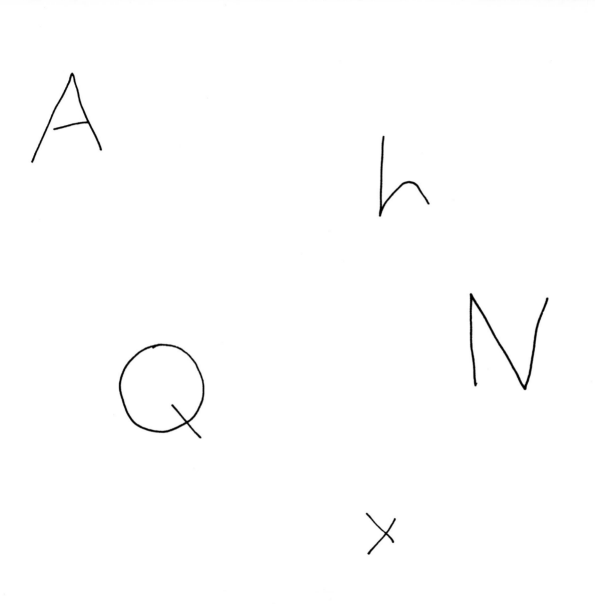

F

b

F

M

Y

v

C

i

K

s

W

d

G

P

r

Z

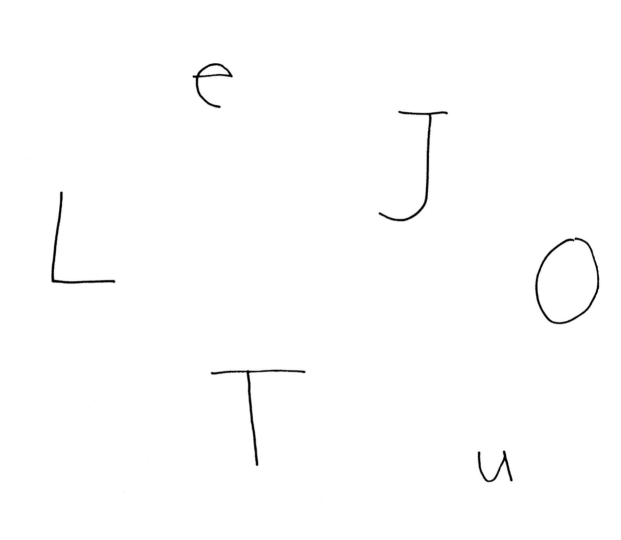

A a B b C c D d E e
F f G g H h I i J j
K k L l M m N n O o
P p Q q R r S s T t U u
V v W w X x Y y Z z

A a B b C c D d E e

F f G g H h I i J j

K k L l M m N n O o

P p Q q R r S s T t U u

V v W w X x Y y Z z